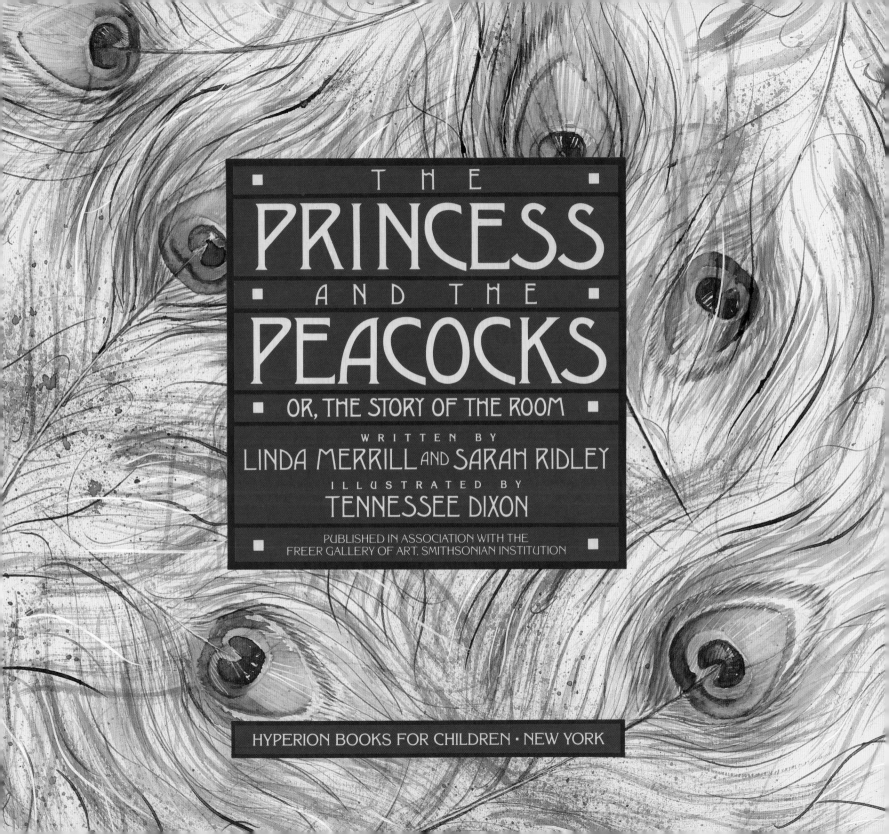

THE PRINCESS AND THE PEACOCKS

OR, THE STORY OF THE ROOM

WRITTEN BY
LINDA MERRILL AND SARAH RIDLEY

ILLUSTRATED BY
TENNESSEE DIXON

PUBLISHED IN ASSOCIATION WITH THE
FREER GALLERY OF ART, SMITHSONIAN INSTITUTION

HYPERION BOOKS FOR CHILDREN · NEW YORK

Text © 1993 by Smithsonian Institution.
Illustrations © 1993 by Tennessee Dixon. All rights reserved.
Printed in Italy.
For information address Hyperion Books for Children,
114 Fifth Avenue, New York, New York 10011.
FIRST EDITION
1 3 5 7 9 10 8 6 4 2

Library of Congress Cataloging-in-Publication Data
Merrill, Linda, 1959–
The princess and the peacocks, or, The story of the Room/written
by Linda Merrill [and] Sarah Ridley; illustrated by Tennessee
Dixon — 1st ed.
p. cm.
Summary: A princess in a portrait by the famous American painter
James McNeill Whistler tells how he transforms the dreary room
where she hangs in his wealthy patron's house in London into the
spectacular Peacock Room.
"Published in association with the Freer Gallery of Art,
Smithsonian Institution."
ISBN 1-56282-327-2 (trade) — ISBN 1-56282-328-0 (lib. bdg.)
1. Peacock Room — Juvenile fiction.   2. Whistler, James McNeill,
1843–1903 — Juvenile fiction.   [1. Peacock Room — Fiction.
2. Whistler, James McNeill, 1834–1903 — Fiction.]   I. Ridley, Sarah.
II. Dixon, Tennessee, ill.   III. Title.   IV. Title: Story of the
Room.
mi7.M54537Pr   1993
[Fic] — dc20   92-72019   CIP   AC

The artwork for each picture is prepared in pen and ink and watercolors.
This book is set in 14-point Cochin.
Photos by John Tsantes and Jeffrey Crespi. Copyright © 1993 Smithsonian Institution.
Design by Karen Palinko.

Once upon a time, about a hundred years ago, I reigned over the dining room of an old house in London.

From my place above the mantel, I looked down upon the dreary room. The walls were covered with yellowish leather adorned with a pattern of tired flowers. Blue-and-white china plates and pots sat on dark wooden shelves, and a faded Turkish carpet lay on the floor. Eight gas lamps hung from a gloomy ceiling. It was a horrible place, and I couldn't bear the thought of living there forever.

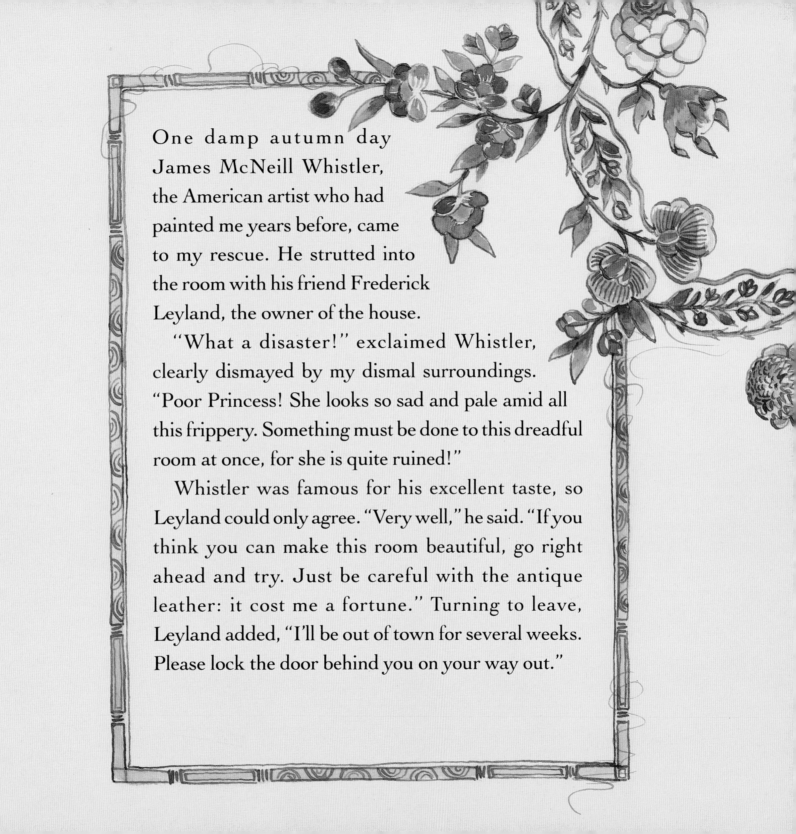

One damp autumn day James McNeill Whistler, the American artist who had painted me years before, came to my rescue. He strutted into the room with his friend Frederick Leyland, the owner of the house.

"What a disaster!" exclaimed Whistler, clearly dismayed by my dismal surroundings. "Poor Princess! She looks so sad and pale amid all this frippery. Something must be done to this dreadful room at once, for she is quite ruined!"

Whistler was famous for his excellent taste, so Leyland could only agree. "Very well," he said. "If you think you can make this room beautiful, go right ahead and try. Just be careful with the antique leather: it cost me a fortune." Turning to leave, Leyland added, "I'll be out of town for several weeks. Please lock the door behind you on your way out."

As soon as we heard the click of the front door closing, Whistler let out a piercing laugh, as shrill as a peacock's cry.

"He's gone!" he cried gleefully. "Now I can make this room fit for you, the Princess from the Land of Porcelain."

Whistler bowed deeply to me, then briefly left the room. He returned with scissors and paints and set to work trimming the red border from the rug. Next he picked up a paintbrush and approached the walls. I wanted to cry out in alarm but could only observe in silence as Whistler covered the red flowers on Leyland's leather, one by one, with dabs of yellow paint.

As he retouched the final rose, the artist winked at me and said, "You're looking better already, Princess. But something is still missing...." Muttering to himself, he turned out the lights and walked out the door.

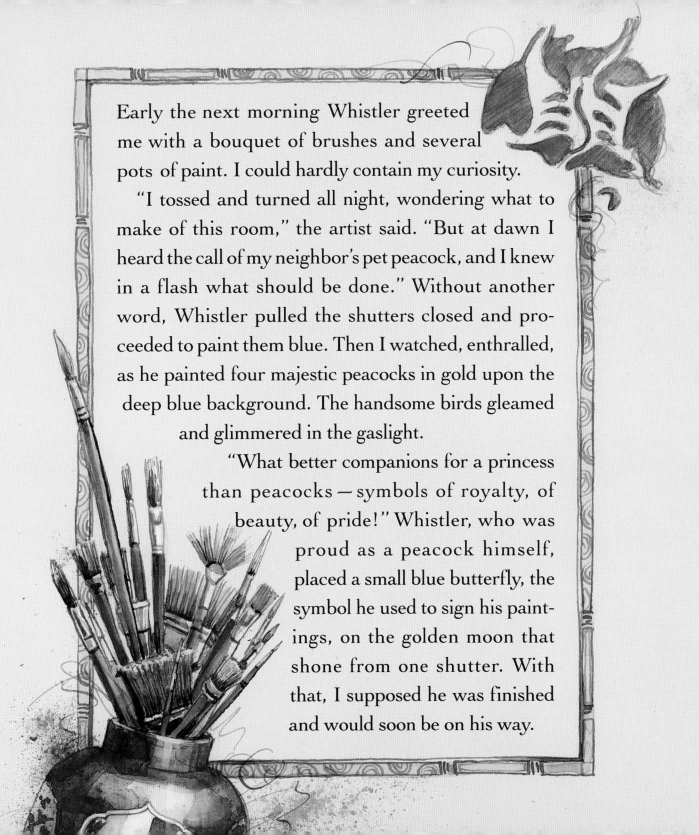

Early the next morning Whistler greeted me with a bouquet of brushes and several pots of paint. I could hardly contain my curiosity.

"I tossed and turned all night, wondering what to make of this room," the artist said. "But at dawn I heard the call of my neighbor's pet peacock, and I knew in a flash what should be done." Without another word, Whistler pulled the shutters closed and proceeded to paint them blue. Then I watched, enthralled, as he painted four majestic peacocks in gold upon the deep blue background. The handsome birds gleamed and glimmered in the gaslight.

"What better companions for a princess than peacocks — symbols of royalty, of beauty, of pride!" Whistler, who was proud as a peacock himself, placed a small blue butterfly, the symbol he used to sign his paintings, on the golden moon that shone from one shutter. With that, I supposed he was finished and would soon be on his way.

To my surprise, Whistler strung up a hammock in a corner of the room, as though he wanted to take a nap. But when he lay down, he gazed intently at the lamps drooping from the ceiling. Suddenly he sprang up and fetched a ladder, which he climbed to the very top. With his hair nearly dusting the lamps, he fixed tiny sheets of gold onto the ceiling. When he laughed too loudly or sneezed hard, the delicate squares crumbled and fell like snow. His clothes and his curls were soon sprinkled with golden flakes.

When Whistler had completed his work, I felt as though the room were full of sunshine, even though the shutters remained tightly closed.

Whistler then tied his longest brush to the end of his walking stick and, reclining in the hammock, painted a shimmering pattern of peacock feathers all over the golden ceiling.

"Utterly gorgeous!" he cried at last. "I've made this room alive with beauty, refined to the last degree!" I considered my newly painted room charming indeed but wondered whether it was quite what Leyland had in mind.

Every day Whistler added something new. Before long there were peacock feathers everywhere, and the room became the talk of London. Friends and artists came to call, eager to see the wonders Whistler was working in Leyland's house.

One morning, Leyland returned.

"Whistler!" he exclaimed in surprise. "Look what you've done! Birds on the windows, flowers on the walls, feathers on the ceiling — it's dreadful!"

Attempting to smooth his patron's ruffled feathers, Whistler explained, "Now, Leyland. As a man of excellent taste, you must agree that these magnificent peacocks make perfect companions for the Princess."

Leyland did not agree. "Just tell me what I owe you," he said angrily, "and then be on your way."

With scarcely a pause the artist replied, "Two thousand golden guineas. The shutters alone are worth twelve hundred."

"Two thousand guineas!" Leyland spluttered. "That's much more money than I had in mind and far more than I'm willing to pay! As for peacocks: they're disagreeable birds, and I have no need for them in my house. Take the shutters with you, if you must, but I refuse to pay what you demand!"

As Leyland ranted, Whistler fell silent. Finally, sounding unusually meek, the artist said: "Very well, Leyland. We shall split the cost of this disaster. You pay me one thousand guineas as your share, and I, for mine, will continue working here — at no further expense to you — until I've brought harmony to this room."

Still grumbling, but satisfied that the problem would soon be solved, Leyland shook hands with Whistler and took his leave. As soon as he had gone, Whistler turned to me and vowed, "I'll make him sorry he ever spoke ill of peacocks!"

Whistler arrived later than usual the next morning, pushing a trolley full of overflowing pails of paint.

"Farewell, roses," Whistler sang as he dipped his brush into the paint.

"Farewell, pansies," as he drew it out again.

"Farewell, chrysanthemums," as he swept thick strokes of peacock blue over the walls.

Singing and laughing all the while, Whistler painted as he never had before. I watched in wonder as Leyland's costly leather disappeared before my very eyes.

Then Whistler turned his back to me and fixed his stare on the blank blue wall. All at once he picked up his brush and went to work. By morning a pair of golden peacocks, frozen in a quarrel, had been painted on the wall.

The bird that fanned its tail feathers was pushy and proud. Gold and silver coins showered from its outspread wings and scattered onto the ground at its feet. On its throat were silver feathers, which looked rather like the ruffles on a shirt.

The other peacock, whose tail swept bare ground, appeared poor and put-upon. Crowning its head was a single silver feather, which looked rather like a lock of white hair.

Thrilled with his achievement, Whistler took to entertaining guests with picnic suppers, served by the light of the flickering lamps beneath a sky of peacock feathers.

One day another princess (not nearly as lovely as I) paid a visit to my room. "How exquisite," she remarked. "Did you consult Mr. Leyland about your scheme of decoration?"

"Why should I?" Whistler haughtily replied. "I'm creating the most beautiful work of art in the world!"

Whistler also invited reporters to the Peacock Room, as they called it. Soon the newspapers were full of praise for his work. Realizing the publicity might bring Leyland back to London, Whistler spent one last night making sure every peacock feather was perfectly in place. At dawn he returned Leyland's blue-and-white pots to the glittering shelves and sighed with satisfaction. "Now then, Princess," Whistler said with a contented smile, "you shall live happily ever after in this splendid Land of Porcelain."

He turned to take a final look at the fighting peacocks, whose diamond and sapphire eyes flashed in the firelight. "Amazing," he said. With a final courtly bow, he left my room, a glorious harmony in blue and gold, and locked the door behind him. I never saw Whistler, or he the Peacock Room, again.

Leyland came home the very next day. "What has become of my valuable leather?" he cried, staring in disbelief at the peacock blue walls. But when he noticed me, framed in gold and surrounded by gleaming vases, Leyland gasped in astonishment, as if seeing me for the very first time. "Whistler has indeed made you the Princess of Peacocks and Porcelains," he said. "This room is truly yours, not mine."

Leyland was correct, of course. I now felt entirely at home in my place above the mantel, looking out upon the most beautiful room in all the world.

Every evening for the rest of his life, as Leyland sat at the head of his dining room table, he was forced to face the peacocks Whistler had painted on the wall. Sometimes I would catch him turning his eyes from the pair of quarrelsome birds; and although he never said so to me, I feel certain he was sorry he had ever spoken ill of peacocks.

The Princess from the Land of Porcelain still reigns over Whistler's *Harmony in Blue and Gold: The Peacock Room.* You will find the Princess and the peacocks in the Freer Gallery of Art in Washington, D.C., where they remain as Whistler left them, once upon a time.